Lend Me Your Wings

The author wishes to thank Richard Callanan who commissioned this story for BBC Television's 'You and Me', and Ruth Creek for her editorial help with the text.

Text copyright © 1987 by John Agard
Illustrations copyright © 1987 by Adrienne Kennaway

First U.S. edition

First published in Great Britain in 1987

Library of Congress Cataloging-in-Publication Data

Agard, John, 1949–
      Lend me your wings/by John Agard; illustrated
by Adrienne Kennaway. — 1st ed.
            p.   cm.
      Summary: A fish who longs to fly and a bird who
longs to swim trade fins and wings for a new look
at life.
      ISBN 0-316-02010-9
      [1. Fishes — Fiction. 2. Birds — Fiction.]
I. Moore, Adrienne, ill. II. Title.
PZ7.A26197Le 1988
[E] — dc19   88-10920
                                                   CIP
                                                   AC

10   9   8   7   6   5   4   3   2   1

Printed in Belgium

Lend Me Your Wings

Words by **John Agard**
Pictures by **Adrienne Kennaway**

Little, Brown and Company
Boston   Toronto

On a happy crick-crack morning
when wind gives leaves
a small shiver

Sister Fish swam up
to the top of a river
and saw the tall trees
green in the air

Sister Fish saw the sun
a shining yellow rock

Sister Fish saw the clouds
white moss drifting up there

"If only I could have a swim
in all that blue,"
Sister Fish thought
as she looked up at the sky

Trees waved at her
Sky gazed at her
Sun smiled at her

But Sister Fish
could only look and wish

From his branch above the river
Brother Bird watching the water
so full of sky
and the sun shimmering
like a great golden egg

"If only I could fly
into that other sky,"
Brother Bird thought
as he looked down at the water

Brother Bird hopped down
to a big rock in the river
and Sister Fish could see his two wings
making flutters in the breeze
of the crick-crack morning

"That's just what I need,"
Sister Fish said to herself.
"Wings to take me as high as I please."

So she swam up to Brother Bird
and said, "Please lend me your wings
I'd really like to see what up there is like."
Sister Fish gave one flick-tail towards the sky

"And I'd really like to see what down there is like,"
Brother Bird said
and he gave one flick-wing towards the river

"Well, I can always lend you my fins,"
Sister Fish said

Brother Bird agreed
and in quick-wink time he took off his wings

Sister Fish did the same with her fins

And so from the cool of the rock
the two of them set out
Sister Fish with Brother Bird wings
Brother Bird with Sister Fish fins

What a sweet fun feeling
on a crick-crack morning!

For Sister Fish it's a new feel of wings
a flying upwards thrill

For Brother Bird it's a new feel of fins
a fun-time turn in water

See Brother Bird do a dive thing
from a floating coconut

Imagine one fisherman seeing this bird playing fish!

Now Sister Fish taking a first-time look at mango tree

See her fish-eye gleam with big surprise
to see a kiskadee bird picking at bright mango

Kis-kis-ka-dee Kis-kis-ka-dee

Sister Fish tried to make that same sound too
as she went higher into the blue

Now Brother Bird playing hide-and-seek
with hairy-leg crab
and pink-shell shrimp

See his bird-eye shine with big surprise
to see dazzle-skin water snake

Brother Bird knew many worms
but none as fat as dazzle-skin water snake

Now Sister Fish seeing
something with a long dancing tail
buzzing in the wind

A kite!

And on that crick-crack morning
one child with a kite
could go home and say
"I see a fish playing bird today."

But right now the big winds coming
Sister Fish could feel the wings at her side
becoming much too heavy.
She tried to keep up her gliding

but all of a sudden
she found herself falling
and falling
and falling and the sky turning
and turning
and turning
in her head

With a plop
Sister Fish landed
right back in the river
and there was her friend Brother Bird
                    beating his fins
            till he was just a blur of a thing
                    hurrying to the rock
                    but hardly moving
                    and breathing hard
            just like Sister Fish herself

"I'm glad to see you," Brother Bird said.
"Thank you back for my wings
and you can have back your fins.
I think sky is best for me after all."

"And I'm glad to see you too," Sister Fish said.
"Thank you back for my fins
I think water is best for me after all."

So Brother Bird took back his wings
and Sister Fish took back her fins

They told each other goodbye
and one made a dive for the river
and the other headed for the sky

But something happened
to Sister Fish and Brother Bird

A true wonder of a thing!

From that crick-crack morning
Brother Bird began to fly in a very special way

He would kind of dip-dip his wing
forever playing as if he was under water
and move his feathers like tiny waves

The other birds wondered how he did it.

And as for Sister Fish
well, she wasn't happy just to swim

Every now and then she would skim-skim
over the water
as if she was heading for the sky

The other fish wondered how she did it.

Only Sister Fish and Brother Bird know the secret.
Only Sister Fish and Brother Bird have the answer.